The Seahorses

Move out of Coral City

Writen by: Sandra Rivera Sánchez

Illustrations: Muuaaa

Made in
Puerto Rico

The Seahorses Move Out Of Coral City

ISBN-13: 978-0-578-45657-7
First Edition: 2019
© Text: Sandra Rivera Sánchez
© Ilustration and design: Muuaaa Design Studio
© Edition: Palmira Isabel Rojas
Translated by: Walter Irizarry

To contact the author, you may write to
caballitosdemar2018@gmail.com or visit the facebook page
@los caballitos de mar se mudan del coral

Printed in Colombia: Ladiprint Editorial

...to those that choose to dream and
with that energy reach for the stars...

"once upon a time"...

that's how my grandpa began
telling me every story...

♪ ...at the edge of the deep blue sea, life was full of peace and happiness in a reef called Coral City. Colorful fish strolled about and seahorses danced around the beautiful coral reef.

But one day, cans and plastic bags were falling from up above. More and more garbage rained on Coral City! Mr. Don, a strong seahorse that guarded the Seaweed Parks, noticed Riley and her brother Hank were in trouble and went to their rescue.

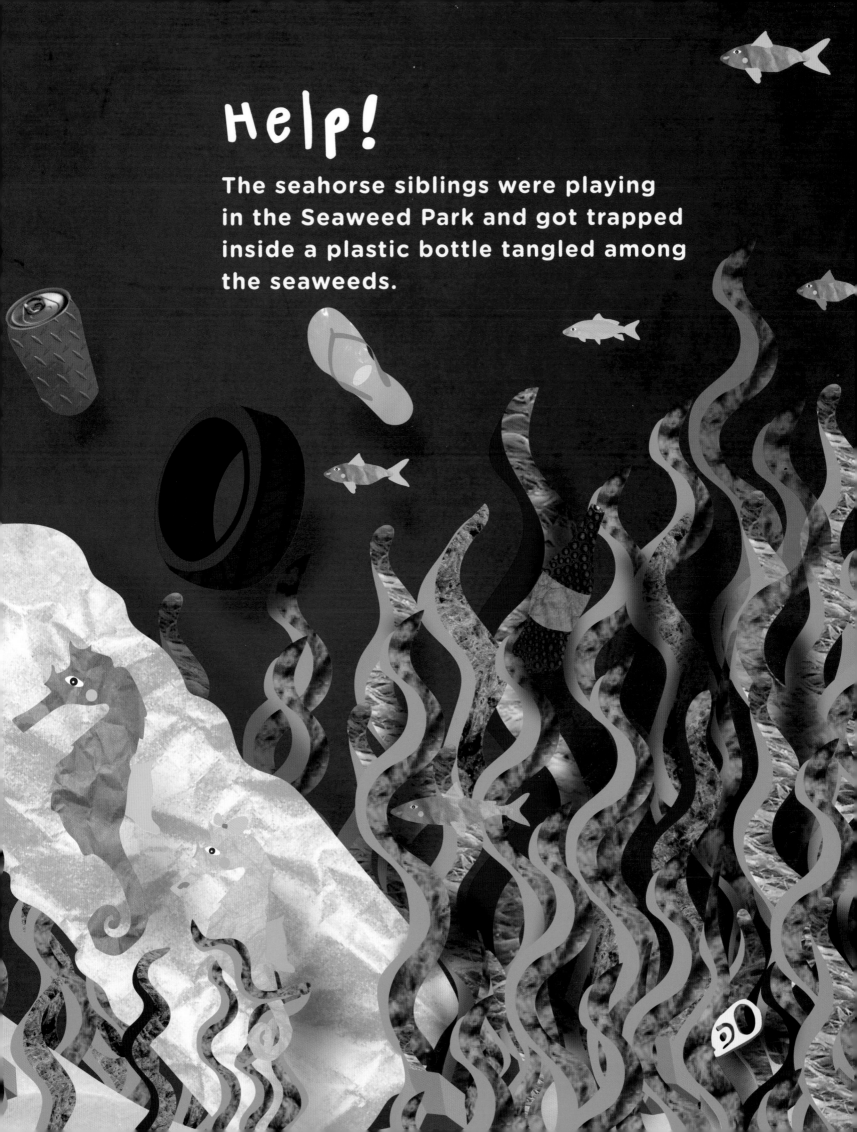

Help!

The seahorse siblings were playing in the Seaweed Park and got trapped inside a plastic bottle tangled among the seaweeds.

BOOM!

Strange objects kept falling from up above; bottle caps, drinking straws, plastic bags, even a car tire. This worried Mr. Don, so he paid a visit to the city mayor, a spiky black sea urchin called Antilles.

"Mayor Antilles, we have to do something about all the garbage that's burying our city!" said Mr. Don.

"I will ask all families to help collect the garbage from the reef and return it to the beach. Let's ask Riley and Hank to help us spread the message" replied the mayor.

Riley and Hank were quick to help. They went to find Miss Cushy, the starfish that ran the newspaper The Wave. She was a great reporter.

The Wave

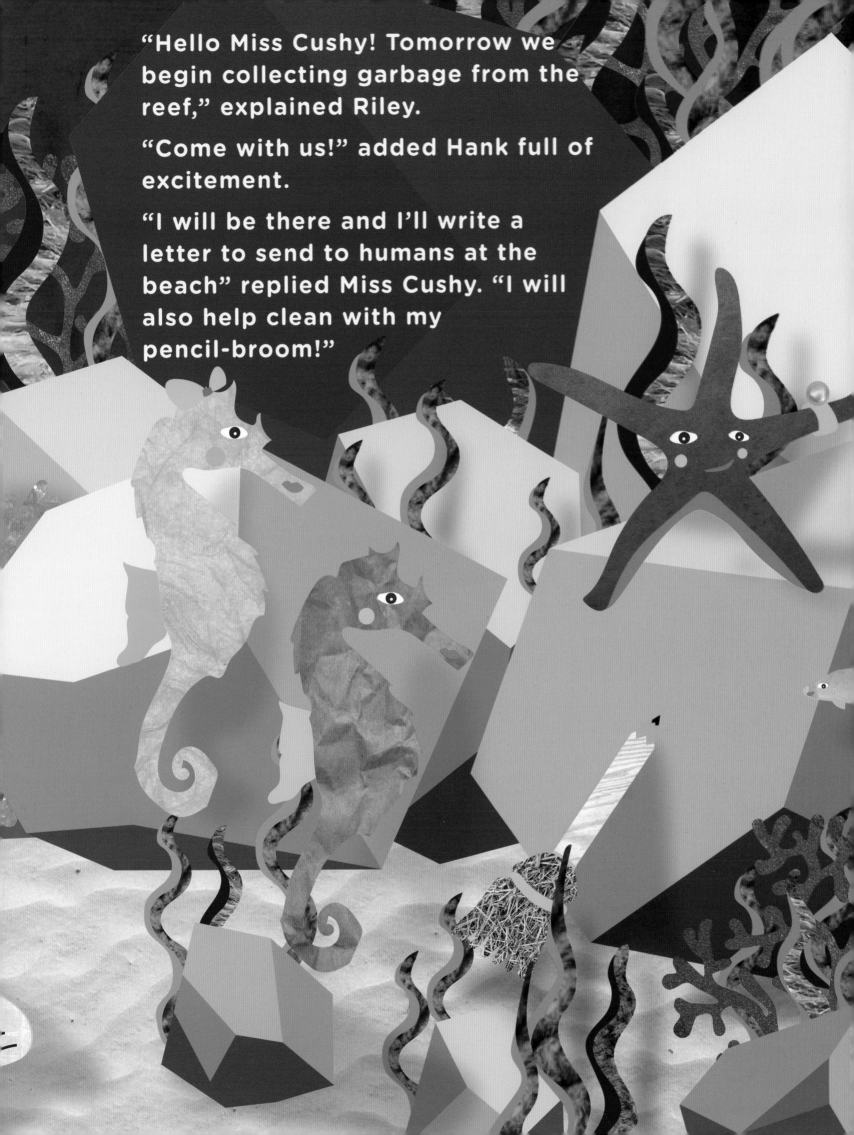

"Hello Miss Cushy! Tomorrow we begin collecting garbage from the reef," explained Riley.

"Come with us!" added Hank full of excitement.

"I will be there and I'll write a letter to send to humans at the beach" replied Miss Cushy. "I will also help clean with my pencil-broom!"

Clean up day arrived and while everyone was helping to collect all the garbage, they heard a loud splashing getting closer and closer and...

CRaSH!

Young people were snorkeling around the reef and their boat anchor had landed on the rooftop of the Coral City School. They were stepping right on the coral with their long rubber flippers!

Mayor Antilles gathered everyone and announced, "Sadly, we all have to move to a different coral reef. But, not without finishing our clean-up project and sending our letter!"

And that's exactly what they did.

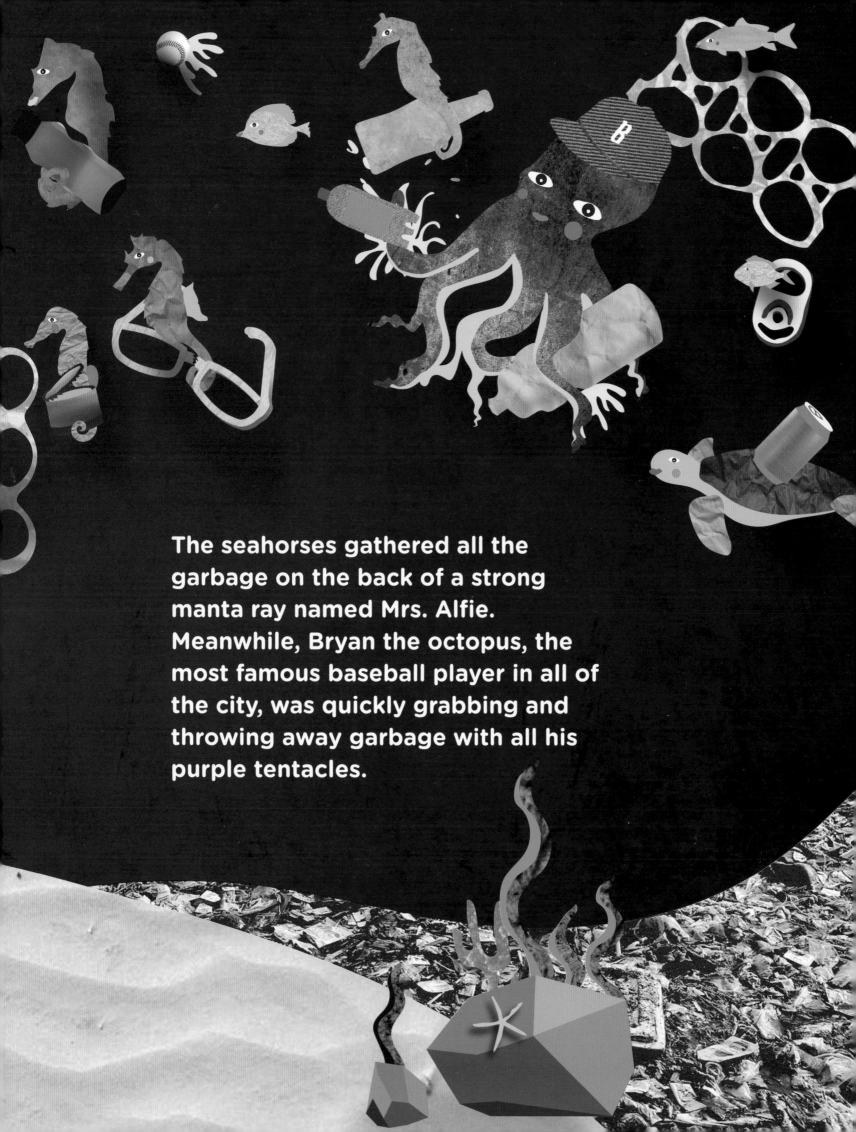

The seahorses gathered all the garbage on the back of a strong manta ray named Mrs. Alfie. Meanwhile, Bryan the octopus, the most famous baseball player in all of the city, was quickly grabbing and throwing away garbage with all his purple tentacles.

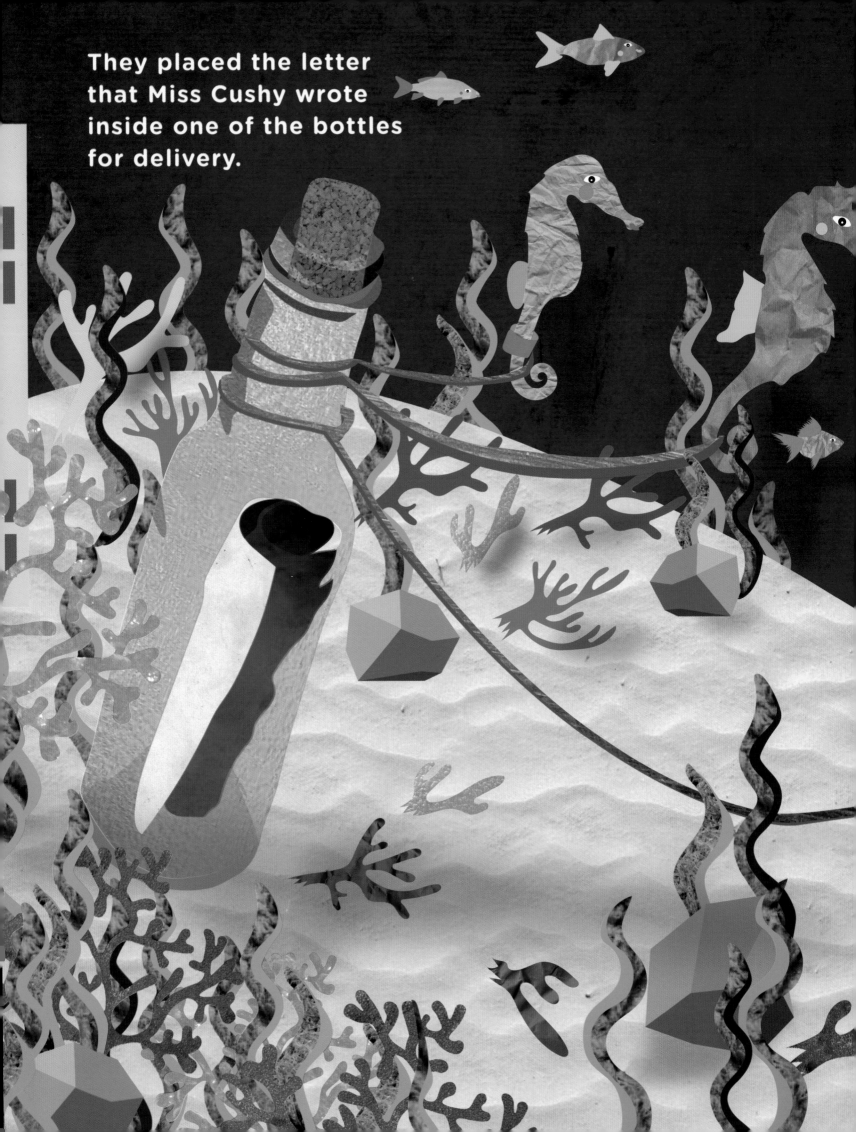

They placed the letter
that Miss Cushy wrote
inside one of the bottles
for delivery.

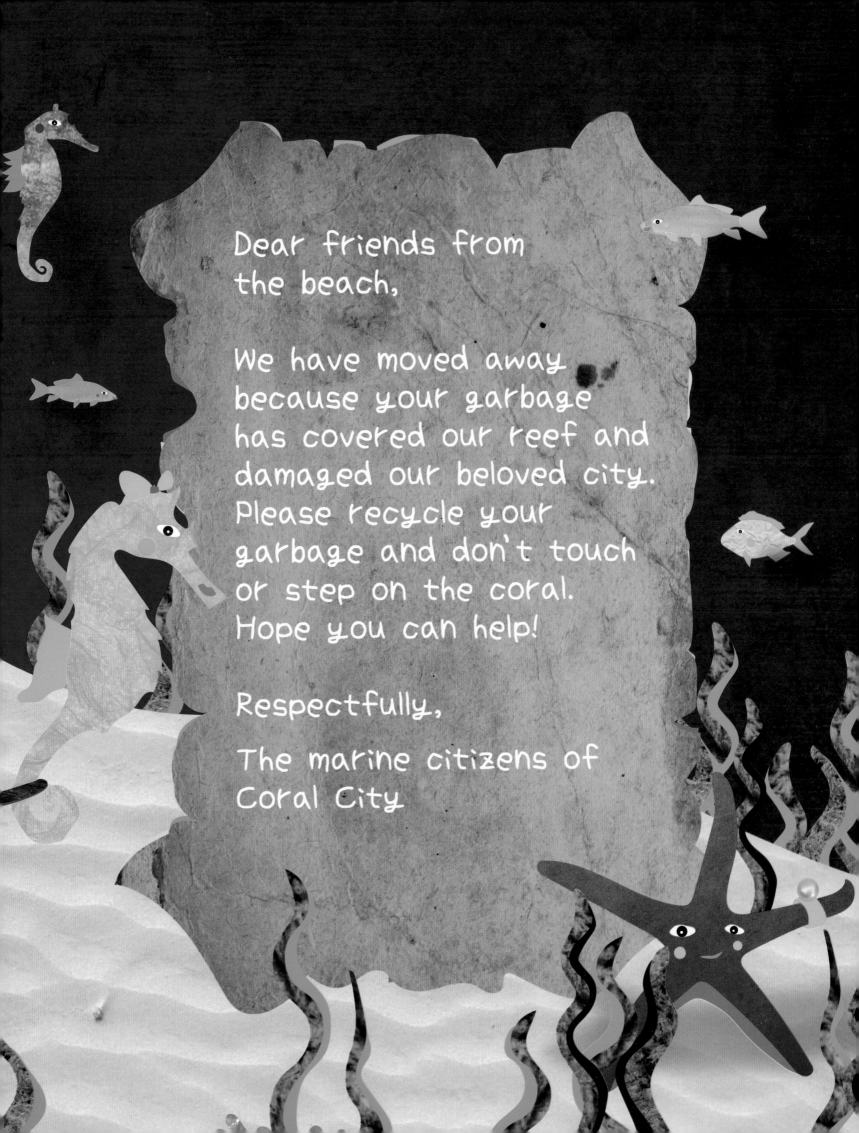

Dear friends from
the beach,

We have moved away
because your garbage
has covered our reef and
damaged our beloved city.
Please recycle your
garbage and don't touch
or step on the coral.
Hope you can help!

Respectfully,

The marine citizens of
Coral City

Riley and Hank swam with their family to a different coral reef called Deep Blue City, a little further away from the beach.

SPLaSH!

One day while playing at a Seaweed Park, they spotted a girl wearing a pink diving mask. She was floating above the reef and dove under water with a sign that read:

we are reusing and recycling now!
We have learned to be careful to never touch or step on the coral.

And suddenly, a little boy with big cheeks full of air and a floaty around his belly, sank another sign that read: "We love you!" And everyone in Deep Blue City lived joyfully ever after!

Curious facts about seahorses:

- Seahorses swim upright (like standing up) propelling themselves by using their dorsal fin.

- Their eyes move independently of each other like those of a chameleon.

- They have long snouts, which they use to suck up food.

- Seahorses don't have stomachs, therefore they must eat constantly to stay alive.

- They are one of the slowest moving ocean creatures.

- The crown-like spikes on their heads are all different, unique, much like a fingerprint.

- They can camouflage themselves by changing colors depending on their habitat.

- The female seahorse will deposit her eggs in the male seahorse, who will carry the eggs until they hatch.

Sandra Rivera Sánchez was born in the beautiful island of Puerto Rico, on December 3, 1971. During her elementary school years, she enjoyed writing letters to friends all over the world through an English program called Pen Pals, where her love for writing started. She studied marketing at The University of Puerto Rico and worked many years as a Media Director for an international advertising company until her first child was born. Married to Eng. Carlos Sierra Del Llano III, a sailor and a nature lover as she is, Sandra started a new journey as a yoga and meditation teacher specialized in yoga for children. Snorkeling with Carlos and their two kids, she got inspired to write her first book for children about protecting our oceans and reefs through recycling. She always carries a pencil and a special notebook wherever she goes, so she can set free her lifelong passion for writing.